W9-BNO-358

This book belongs to:

CHARLOTTE

Published by Ladybird Books Ltd
80 Strand London WC2R 0RL
A Penguin Company

13 15 17 19 20 18 16 14

© LADYBIRD BOOKS LTD MCMXCVIII

LADYBIRD and the device of a Ladybird are trademarks of Ladybird Books Ltd
All rights reserved. No part of this publication may be reproduced,
stored in a retrieval system, or transmitted in any form or by any
means, electronic, mechanical, photocopying, recording or otherwise,
without the prior consent of the copyright owner.

Printed in Italy

Rapunzel

illustrated by Peter Stevenson

Ladybird

One day, a man and his wife were walking past a witch's garden. They were so hungry that they took some of the witch's lettuce.

Soon, they were hungry again, and the man went to the witch's garden for more lettuce. But this time, the witch saw him.

"You will be punished for taking my lettuce," said the witch. "I will take your first baby away from you."

Not long after, the man and his wife had a baby girl. The witch came and took her away.

"I will call you Rapunzel," she said.

The witch locked Rapunzel high up in a tower. The tower had no door, just one window, for Rapunzel to look out.

11

Every day, the witch came to see Rapunzel.

She called up to the window, "Rapunzel, Rapunzel, let down your hair."

And Rapunzel threw her long, golden hair out of the window for the witch to climb up.

One day, a prince was walking past the tower. He heard a girl singing, and saw Rapunzel at the window.

Then the witch came.

The Prince heard her call to Rapunzel, and saw her climb up Rapunzel's golden hair.

After the witch had gone away, the Prince went to the tower and called, "Rapunzel, Rapunzel, let down your hair."

And Rapunzel threw her golden hair out of the window for the Prince to climb up.

The Prince and Rapunzel talked for a very long time.

The Prince said, "You are too beautiful to be locked up all alone. I will help you to escape."

The next day, the witch
came to see Rapunzel.
As she was climbing up,
the witch hurt Rapunzel.

"Ouch!" said Rapunzel.
"The Prince did not hurt
me as he climbed up."

The witch was very angry.
To punish Rapunzel, the
witch cut off all her
beautiful hair.

The next day, the Prince went to see Rapunzel again.

He called up to the window, "Rapunzel, Rapunzel, let down your hair." And he waited.

Soon, Rapunzel's beautiful golden hair came down from the window, and the Prince climbed up.

To his surprise, the witch
was waiting at the window.
She threw the Prince from
the tower.

29

As he fell, the Prince hurt his eyes on some thorns.

"Help!" he cried. "I cannot see." Rapunzel wanted to help the Prince, but the witch took her away.

The Prince went everywhere searching for Rapunzel, but he couldn't find her.

Then one day, the Prince heard a girl singing.

"Rapunzel," he cried. "Is it you?"

"Yes," said Rapunzel.

Rapunzel was so happy to see the Prince that she started to cry. Her tears fell into the Prince's eyes, and all at once, he could see again.

Rapunzel said that the witch was dead. She would never be locked up in the tower ever again. She had been singing because she was so happy.

The Prince took Rapunzel away to his palace. Very soon, they were married, and everyone talked happily of the Princess Rapunzel.

So Rapunzel and her prince
lived happily ever after.

Read It Yourself is a series of graded readers designed to give young children a confident and successful start to reading.

Level 3 is suitable for children who are developing reading confidence and stamina, and who are ready to progress to longer stories with a wider vocabulary. The stories are told simply and with a richness of language.

About this book

At this stage of reading development, it's rewarding to ask children how they prefer to approach each new story. Some children like to look first at the pictures and discuss them with an adult. Some children prefer the adult to read the story to them before they attempt it for themselves. Many children at this stage will be eager to read the story aloud to an adult at once, and to discuss it afterwards. Unknown words can be worked out by looking at the beginning letter (*what sound does this letter make?*) and the sounds the child recognises within the word. The child can then decide which word would make sense.

Developing readers need lots of praise and encouragement.